P9-DGW-450

Schnitzel von Krumm's
Basketwork

Lynley Dodd

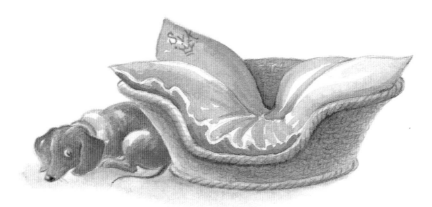

Gareth Stevens Publishing
A WORLD ALMANAC EDUCATION GROUP COMPANY

Tucked in a hideyhole
under the stair,
lay a rickety basket
in need of repair;
a chewed-up old cushion,
a blanket all worn,
everything broken
and smelly
and torn.
AND . . .
under the blanket,
his paws on his tum,
happily snoring,
lay Schnitzel von Krumm.

He liked all the tatters,
he liked every tear,
the broken-down edges,
the holes, and the hair.
The smell was so friendly,
and as for the fit –
if he needed to squeeze,
did he mind?
Not a bit.
But . . .

"Yuk!" said his family.
"Time to say 'no' –
this beaten-up basket
must INSTANTLY go.
It's scruffy
and dirty,
it's hopelessly small,
and we really can't have
such a smell
in the hall."
So they lifted the basket
and took it away
and bought him another
the very same day.

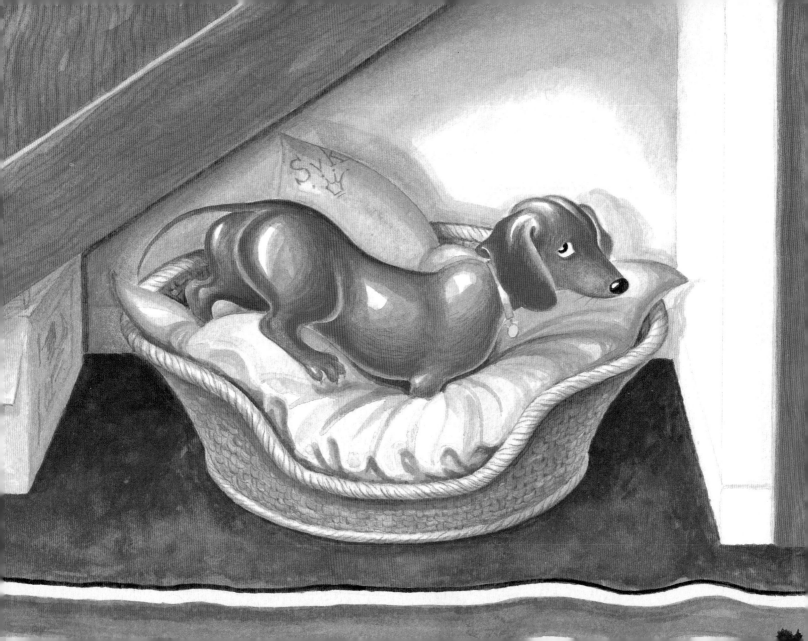

He tried it for size,
there was room for his tum;
but it didn't smell friendly
to Schnitzel von Krumm.
The basket was stylish,
a much better fit –
was it cozy and comforting?
NO,
not a bit.

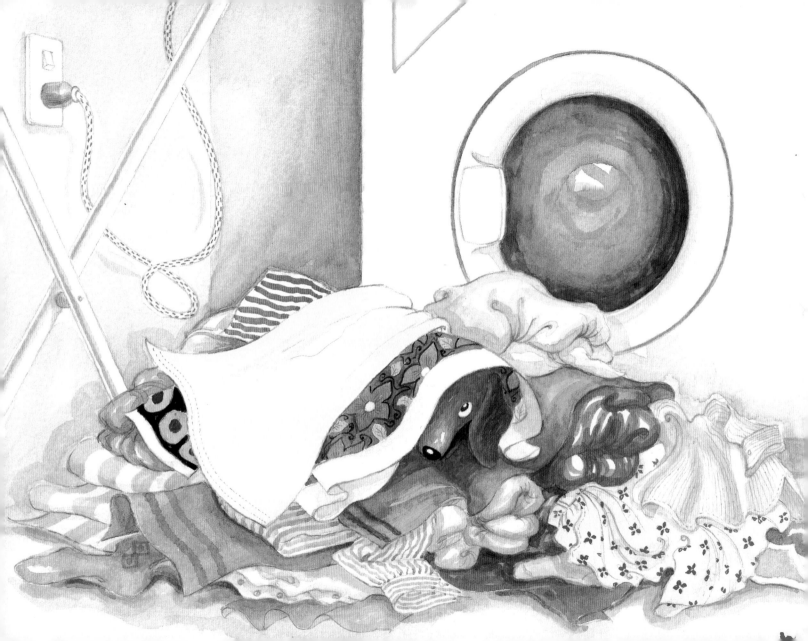

He made a new bed
in a jumble of shirts,
pajamas and towels,
and flowery skirts.
But
something was wrong
with the smell
and the fit;
was it cozy and comforting?

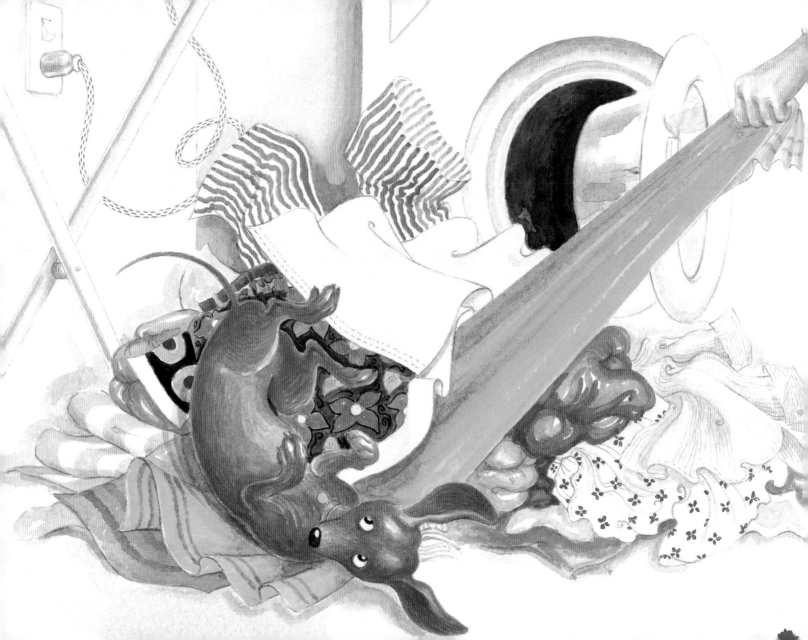

NO,
not a bit.

APPLES

He made a new bed
with the dusters and mops,
the cleaners and brooms,
and preserving-jar tops.
But
something was wrong
with the smell
and the fit;
was it cozy and comforting?

NO,
not a bit.

He made a new bed
in a rack full of greens,
with the spinach and celery,
parsley and beans.
But
something was wrong
with the smell
and the fit;
was it cozy and comforting?

NO,
not a bit.

He made a new bed
at the side of the shed,
in the daisies and dahlias,
yellow and red.
But
something was wrong
with the smell
and the fit;
was it cozy and comforting?

NO,
not a bit.

Poor Schnitzel von Krumm.
He sat on the stair
and dreamed of his basket,
the holes, and the hair.
The broken-down edges,
the blanket all worn,
everything scruffy
and smelly
and torn.
His ears drooped down,
and his tail did, too.
"HELP!" said his family.
"What can we DO?"

So . . .
back to the hideyhole
under the stair,
went the battered old basket
in need of repair.
And back in a hurry
went Schnitzel von Krumm,
with a wag of his tail
and a heave of his tum.
The new one was stylish,
a MUCH better fit –
but when it had gone,
did he mind?

NOT A BIT!

Please visit our web site at: **www.garethstevens.com**
For a free color catalog describing Gareth Stevens' list of high-quality books and multimedia programs, call 1-800-542-2595 (USA) or 1-800-461-9120 (Canada). Gareth Stevens Publishing's Fax: (414) 332-3567.

Other GOLD STAR FIRST READER
Millennium Editions:

A Dragon in a Wagon
Find Me a Tiger
Hairy Maclary from Donaldson's Dairy
Hairy Maclary Scattercat
Hairy Maclary, Sit
Hairy Maclary and Zachary Quack
Hairy Maclary's Bone
Hairy Maclary's Caterwaul Caper
Hairy Maclary's Rumpus at the Vet
Slinky Malinki
Slinky Malinki, Open the Door
The Smallest Turtle
SNIFF-SNUFF-SNAP!
Wake Up, Bear

and also by Lynley Dodd:

Hairy Maclary's Showbusiness
The Minister's Cat ABC
Schnitzel von Krumm Forget-Me-Not
Slinky Malinki Catflaps

Library of Congress Cataloging-in-Publication Data

Dodd, Lynley.
    Schnitzel von Krumm's basketwork / by Lynley Dodd.
        p. cm. — (Gold star first readers)
    Summary: Schnitzel von Krumm is not a happy dog when his well-meaning family replaces his beloved, broken-in basket with an uncomfortable, stylish new one.
        ISBN 0-8368-2783-X (lib. bdg.)
        [1. Dogs—Fiction. 2. Beds—Fiction. 3. Stories in rhyme.]
    I. Title. II. Series.
    PZ8.3.D637Sc 2001
    [E]—dc21   00-063550

This edition first published in 2001 by
Gareth Stevens Publishing
A World Almanac Education Group Company
330 West Olive Street, Suite 100
Milwaukee, WI 53212 USA

First published in New Zealand by Mallinson Rendel Publishers Ltd. Original © 1994 by Lynley Dodd.

All rights reserved. No part of this book may be reproduced, stored in a retrieval system, or transmitted in any form or by any means without permission in writing from Gareth Stevens, Inc.

Printed in Mexico

1 2 3 4 5 6 7 8 9 05 04 03 02 01